ALSO BY ANNE RENWICK

Elemental Web Chronicles

The Golden Spider

The Silver Skull

The Iron Fin

Venomous Secrets

Elemental Web Tales

A Trace of Copper

In Pursuit of Dragons

A Reflection of Shadows

A Snowflake at Midnight

A Ghost in Amber

A Whisper of Bone

Flight of the Scarab

Elemental Web Stories

The Tin Rose

Kraken and Canals

Rust and Steam

KRAKEN AND CANALS

AN ELEMENTAL WEB STORY

ANNE RENWICK

To all kraken enthusiasts

ACKNOWLEDGMENTS

Rossella Marini, a native speaker, for checking my Italian.

Sandra Sookoo, my wonderful editor who mercilessly ferrets out weaknesses and sets my work on a better course.

My husband and my two boys who tolerated my fascination with the foundations of Venice.

My mom and dad who instilled in me a love of both reading and travel.

Mr. Fox and his red pen.

CHAPTER ONE

Venice, Italy
1885

"Hang in there, Gino." Arturo Piatti wound the tourniquet tighter about the man's wrist while struggling to keep his voice calm as his field engineer howled in pain. "Help is on the way."

Overhead, an emergency dirigible transport made rapid progress in their direction over the clay roof tiles of Venice. Gino's hand was badly mangled — far too much blood pooled on the pavement beside the canal. He'd lost a lot more while still in the water.

Crack! The sound of an air rifle tore through the air.

"Nailed him," his sharpshooter announced, though it was small satisfaction. Luigi set aside his weapon to grab a hooked pole and drag the lagoon kraken's limp body — glistening and still twitching — from the foul-smelling canal.

"Indio kraken. Should bring a good price at market. Pay for the doctor."

Jaw clenched, Arturo nodded. Even if it didn't, he would see the bill paid.

Damn kraken. Bane of his existence, they'd stolen too much from him already, including the woman he loved.

Twenty-three years ago he'd proposed. She'd declined. Gently. But her work on the Thames river kraken — her career — took precedence. The resulting wound had never fully healed. Then — half a lifetime later — they'd found each other again. A look. A touch. A whispered flirtation and once again they were love-struck fools.

In the distance, he could make out the roofline of the palazzo where she worked upon a new, mysterious research project. Though another rejection would slay him, he meant to try again.

Soon.

Shoving the ache of old regrets aside, he focused on the job. If not for these miserable cephalopods infesting the canals, his team wouldn't be diving in them to begin with. Walking beside the Venetian canals was dangerous enough, but sending men *into* the canals? *That* required hazard pay.

For decades now, Venice had been plagued by lagoon kraken. In his childhood, the arrival of small squid-like creatures had been largely ignored: a minor nuisance a gondolier could knock off the sides of his craft with an oar. But feeding upon the shellfish that lined the canals, the kraken grew larger. And larger. Until the sharp, claw-like hooks upon the tips of their tentacles began to damage building foundations as they dug into the canal sediment. Not enough to collapse a structure, not yet, though a nearby brick building on the *Rio della Sensa* was dangerously close. Aether help them all if the kraken managed to reach the wooden pilings underneath, the city would begin to crumble.

Such concerns were the reason Arturo had agreed to undertake the design and fabrication of *I Cancelli di Recupero del Canale* — Canal Recovery Gates — that were designed to eliminate the threat kraken posed to Venice. Once the gates were in position, their sharp, spinning blades would operate twice daily, drawing water through the system — slicing and dicing any kraken inhabiting the city's canals — until it was once again safe for gondolas. Though he imagined the canals would be putrid for some time, discouraging pleasure boats, it was a necessary process. From that point forward, the gates could be opened and closed as needed. Installation of the very first gate was nearly complete when disaster struck, irrevocably altering Gino's future.

A sharp whistle drew his attention upward to where a steel gurney lowered on a rope from the rescue dirigible. With Luigi's help, they quickly transferred Gino onto the stretcher, tightly securing the leather buckles. He waved to the medic above, and the gurney lifted. Arturo prayed the surgeons could piece the man's hand back together.

Luigi handed him a rag. "*That* was no accident. I checked the blades before we lowered the gate into the canal. They were perfectly balanced."

"Sabotage," Arturo growled, wiping blood from his

hands before peeling off his dive suit. "And I know exactly who is behind this."

His team had been so close. Every precaution had been taken. Wire grating. A drag net. Even cephalopod-stunning oil had been poured onto the water's surface prior to the installation dive. But in the end, it was human greed that derailed the project and nearly cost a man his life.

Lips pressed into an angry line, Arturo scanned the gawking crowd.

Months ago, word of his project had leaked, raising hope among the populace that the canals of Venice might one day again be navigable. Quietly, a certain British lord had approached him, offering an obscene amount to clear the *Rio della Fornace* — a canal that passed through a formerly rich district of the city — instead of here, in a small, narrow out-of-the-way canal.

But he'd be damned if he'd assist a man who had taken advantage of the kraken infestation to purchase large swaths of Venetian real estate to the detriment of those families who had lived here for generations. Cheap now, those same buildings — adjacent to the Grand Canal — would be invaluable if — when — his project succeeded.

That particular man now leaned against the crumbling stucco of a nearby building, well out of reach of any wandering tentacles. A hint of amusement lit his eyes.

"Lord Garrick," Luigi hissed. "Want me to drop him?" He squinted while he judged the distance, his hands tightening upon the stock of his rifle.

Yes.

"No," Arturo said as loathing welled in his chest. "Too many witnesses." Hands clenched at his sides, he stalked across the short distance, grabbing a fistful of the man's frock coat and dragging him onto his toes. "Why?" he demanded, not bothering to offer him a chance to deny his involvement.

"I did advise you not to begin with this particular canal." Lord Garrick's ever-present and irritating smile slithered upward, twisting the corners of his lips. His dark eyes flashed, eyes that were forever assessing people for an exploitable weakness. Easy to spot the resemblance to his reptilian relatives. "Cease and desist, or suffer the consequences. This is your final warning that any attempts to proceed will have deadly ramifications."

Growling, Arturo shoved him away. "Your soul is no doubt a dark pit to be so completely at ease with destroying a man's life to ensure personal profit."

Smoothing the lapels of his coat, the lord stepped backward, unperturbed. "On the contrary, I seek to save many. A point needed to be made, and if one life was the price..." A shoulder lifted.

"Explain." Arturo braced himself. What kind of twisted justification would be offered?

"Did Lady Judith not enlighten you as to the value of indigo ink?" Lord Garrick's head tipped slightly.

Arturo twitched at the mention of her name. What could she possibly have to do with this?

Lady Judith Ravensburg was a cryptobiologist, famous for her quay-side lectures upon kraken, wherein she scooped baby kraken from the sea to illustrate her points. Often he attended, standing to one side, studying her. A few strands of silver in her dark hair reminded him of the years they'd spent apart, but her figure was still slender and her blue eyes bright. He delighted in her animated presentations on the finer points of The Kraken Controversy. Were the creatures more closely related to squid or octopuses? With features of both, the various hypotheses made for lively debates among kraken enthusiasts.

Afterward, he'd once escorted her to diner wherein they had sampled a variety of squid ink pasta. One particular dish had been colored a strange dark blue. Its flavor was off, however, the bromine salts making it too pungent. Eyebrows raised, he'd asked if she was attempting to poison him for past mistakes.

"On the contrary, indigo kraken ink is rumored to stimulate the immune system." Her eyes had danced. "The species feeds upon the banded dye-murex — a sea snail — known for a purple-blue dye secreted from its hypobrachial gland, a dye which indigo kraken concentrate and chemically alter." He'd gagged, and she'd laughed. "Most can't detect the dibromo-indigotin component, but then again," her voice had dropped to a husky whisper, "you do have a most talented mouth." The air about them had shimmered with heat.

Ink. Kraken. Venice. A wealthy man sponsoring her research. Pieces began to fall in place. In London, her work had drastically reduced the number and size of the Thames river kraken, but here she'd been working to... preserve them? A bitter taste crept into the back of his throat as nausea gripped his stomach.

A low, mocking laugh oozed from Lord Garrick's lungs. "So she hasn't shared a single detail." There was that damned smile again. "Loyal to the core. Loyal to *me*."

His heart gave a great thud. She couldn't... she wouldn't.

"There she is now." Lord Garrick's chin lifted. "Back from Rome."

Arturo turned, catching sight of her dirigible as it made its roof-top landing. "No," he said, shaking his head. "Absolutely not. She does not work for you."

"Ah," Lord Garrick's laugh grated as he turned and strolled away, throwing his last words over his shoulder, "but she does."

CHAPTER TWO

A SALTY WIND RUFFLED the feathers of Lady Judith Ravensdale's hat as she hoisted her skirts and stepped from her dirigible onto the *altare*, a rooftop terrace that served as a landing platform for the palazzo. A burst of noise caught her attention, and — clutching the precious tea canister against her chest — she risked a glance over the edge. Below, a small knot of people gathered beside a narrow canal that branched off the *Rio della Sensa*, waving hands and shouting as a rescue dirigible zipped away. Something had gone dreadfully wrong, and she had a sick feeling she knew exactly what.

Though the indigo kraken clustered in this district held medical promise, they were particularly vicious. She'd warned Lord Garrick, and he had promised *—promised!* — that her research site would be undisturbed by human interference. Her stomach twisted. Not that he held human life in high regard, but she'd thought she could count upon his cooperation so long as he stood to profit financially.

She squinted. Diving equipment was scattered about a work site. A crane crouched at the water's edge, its cable suspending mechanical equipment in the canal. A man stood, hands on hips, glaring upward — at her — while another familiar form sauntered away.

Arturo. Lord Garrick. They'd met?

Not good. Not good at all. Her chest tightened. The timing couldn't possibly be worse. Arturo would want answers, answers she couldn't give him.

Tearing her gaze away, she hurried down the steps into the house. How could this have happened? Here. In this particular canal? To be sure, the canal was small, unnamed and far from the center city. A logical location for him to test his design, but he'd implied his project was months from implementation. Not that she ever pressed for details, not when she couldn't share the particulars of her own. But he longed to restore his city to its former glory.

As lagoon kraken reached their adult size, long, sinuous tentacles began rising from the water, snagging the occasional gondolier by the ankle and dragging him to a watery death. Gondolas were abandoned, shutting down all water traffic. Even crossing a narrow pedestrian bridge was a risky endeavor. Venetians had abandoned their homes in droves, leaving the city a shell of its former self.

Years passed, then one brave — or insane — fisherman netted a number of small kraken that expelled a purplish-blue ink instead of the standard black. He'd sold them to a wealthy gentleman's chef. Soon after consuming *risotto blu con calamari* said gentleman's rosacea had temporarily resolved.

Coincidence? Not at all.

Lord Garrick soon solicited her expertise. Promising her unlimited funding and complete autonomy, he'd managed to lure her to Venice to study this curious new sub-species. Though progress was slow, her experiments indicated that the ink of the indigo kraken possessed both anti-angiogenic and anti-tumorigenic properties.

Unfortunately, a small amount of the processed ink could only treat a malignant tumor, and it was proving near impossible to generate sufficient quantities to bring about a cure. Something she desperately needed now.

Judy paused beside the bedroom door where a black-clad man stood guard. One of her brother's agents. This would not do. "Much as I appreciate the gesture," she began. "You need to blend into the household. Perhaps a footman's uniform."

The look he gave her suggested he'd rather wear a ball gown.

"You're not the only spy about." She flapped her hand. "Go. Find a way to be less conspicuous. And stay *far away* from the steam butler." If Lord Garrick discovered her plans, all was lost.

As the agent slid away, Judy pulled back her shoulders and opened the door. Inside, her Aunt Agatha rested upon a thick feather mattress in an enormous four-poster bed, encapsulated by a canopy and curtains of blue silk. Luxury she quite deserved.

Upon receiving the letter that her sister had died, she had returned to England to raise Judy and her brother — long before his unanticipated succession to a dukedom. She'd swept into their tiny cottage and found Judy tearfully leafing through her mother's sketchbook. So many detailed blueprints and sketches for wondrous contraptions, all sold for mere pounds to support her young children and dissolute husband, earning a pittance while others grew rich from her inventions.

"Do what your mother couldn't," Aunt Agatha had counseled, easing the sketchbook from her hands. "My sister had the most wondrous plans, but implemented none of them. Don't make that mistake." With her aunt's support and encouragement, Judy followed her passion, won a scholarship to Oxford to study cryptozoology and stayed her course, rising to the top of her field and winning the admiration and respect of her peers. Everything that she was today, she owed to her aunt.

"Judith." Aunt Agatha's eyes were bright, but her smile trembled as she stretched out an arm.

Forcing herself to radiate calm confidence, Judy hurried across the room, setting the tea canister on the bedside table. She clasped her aunt's hand, pressing her lips to translucent, paper-thin skin. A stark reminder of an all but inevitable fate.

"The surgery was unsuccessful," her aunt whispered.

"I know." It had been hard to breathe after receiving

such news, even if it was expected. Her aunt had mere weeks.

When Aunt Agatha first complained of a stiffness in her neck that spread down her arm, the summoned doctor waved off her concerns. Then her arm grew weak as a kind of strange numbness took hold.

Judy's brother, the Duke of Avesbury, had pushed mountains aside, ensuring that Aunt Agatha was examined by the best Lister University had to offer. A cervical spinal tumor, furtive and lethal, had wrapped its many tendrils about the central nerve cord and the vertebral artery, strangling the blood supply to her brain. Lord Thornton himself had operated, but removing the entirety of the malignancy proved impossible.

With a lump in her throat, Judy had bent the terms of her contract and informed her brother of one remaining possibility. Arrangements were made, transporting Aunt Agatha to Venice as quickly and as comfortably as possible.

"I *will* see her," Arturo's voice echoed through the palazzo. A moment later, he burst into the bedchamber. Battista, the steam butler, wheeled in behind him, exhorting the intruder to leave. Hair tousled, clothes damp and eyes flashing, Arturo pushed the irritating steambot aside. "Tell me you do not work for Lord Garrick!"

Aether, she loved his passion. His flashing dark eyes and the faint glint of silver at his temples as his broad chest heaved. Still devastatingly handsome at forty-five years. But this was neither the right time nor the right bedchamber to demonstrate the appreciation and regard she held for him.

Heart pounding, she rushed forward and pressed a hand to his mouth, whispering, "Not another word. Please. The butler is not loyal to me."

Arturo inhaled sharply, then froze. His eyes widened — then narrowed — as he took in the occupant of the bed. He fumed, but held his words.

"Battista," she said, dropping her hand and turning to the steam butler. "I will handle this. Please return to your duties and ensure no one else breaches our door."

The butler stopped flapping his hands and made a formal — if creaky — bow. "As you wish."

The faint wisp of steam that leaked from beneath his shirt collar as he rolled away worried Judy. Her niece Olivia had subtly altered his punch card to delay and corrupt portions of the reports of her activities he made to Lord Garrick, but it would have been suspicious if nothing reached his ears.

"What is this all about?" Arturo demanded. "What is *she* doing here?"

"Now, Mr. Piatti." Her aunt's stern voice commanded attention even from what would *not* be her deathbed. "I'll have you know I chided my niece for declining your proposal all those long years ago."

Arturo's eyebrows rose.

"It's true," Judy confessed, her voice a whisper. "I was about to post a letter when I learned of your recent marriage." *To another woman.*

He paled.

But now was not the time to visit the ghosts of their past.

The moment he'd forced his way into the palazzo, time had begun to run through her fingers. Battista's report would reach her patron, and there would be trouble.

"If you'll excuse us, Aunt Agatha." Her aunt needed to rest, not to listen to them quarrel. She led Arturo into the hallway. With the door closed behind them, she took a deep breath and dragged them back to the present. "Lord Garrick's flaws are many, but the research he funds has the potential to help many people."

Arturo threw his hands in the air. "Do not tell me today's disaster is a small price to pay for the advancement of medical science." He pointed a finger, but kept his voice to a low growl. Angry, but respectful of her aunt's rest, he continued. "The man sabotaged my work, injuring a man severely, all to force me to submit to his demands that I clear canals only at his direction."

"What — exactly — happened?" She stood very still, dreading his answer.

As he spoke, her heart slid downward by inches, until it landed in the bottommost pit of her stomach. Incapable of words to describe her distress at this revelation, she wrapped her arms around her waist unable to bring herself to reach for him. Because of her work, a man might have lost his hand.

"Such actions cannot be condoned." Everything was going wrong at once. "I will speak to my assistant Vittoria. We will gather our notes and find another employer." Arturo's stance relaxed. It had been a trial, keeping the details of her research a secret from him but, given Lord Garrick's actions, she no longer felt bound by the non-disclosure agreement she'd signed. "Though there is much to tell you, I must attend to my aunt. Tonight."

"I thought your aunt was receiving treatment in London?" Realization struck. Surprise widened his eyes before sadness crossed his face. "It failed."

A tear slipped down her cheek, and she nodded.

"I'm so sorry." He gathered her rigid form against his chest.

Judy allowed herself to melt into the warmth of his embrace as he smoothed aside a lock of her loose hair. He made her feel safe, if only for a moment. The steps necessary to save her aunt would place her in grave danger. Who in their right mind would willingly enter a giant kraken's den? Did she dare ask for his assistance?

"How can I help?" he murmured into her hair.

Time to find out.

CHAPTER THREE

I T WAS IMPOSSIBLE to stay angry with her. No, not because tears ran down her face, but because she intended to walk away from years of research, from a staggering amount of funding — what other research foundation conducted its work upon ancient rugs beneath Murano glass chandeliers? — simply on his word.

Outrage burned away, leaving behind an ache in his heart. All this time he'd blamed her aunt for Judy's refusal to marry. Instead, Agatha had taken *his* side. It was his own impulsiveness that had robbed him of twenty-three years.

He wouldn't let that happen again. He wasn't going anywhere.

The delight of holding her soft curves against himself was tempered by the circumstances, and by the half laugh that escaped her lips, a sound that held a both a note of pain and relief. Only when they were alone did Judy allow any vulnerability to show and, even then, it was a rare and precious thing. Though he didn't want this moment to end, he could feel the tension building again in her limbs.

Tipping her chin upward, he brushed away a lingering tear and sighed. He recognized the set of her jaw. "I'm not going to like this, am I?"

Not that it mattered. He was hers to command.

When she'd declined his proposal, he'd abandoned England in a temper, returning home to Italy to marry the girl his parents had chosen. Not an unhappy marriage — he had mourned his wife's death — but a piece of his heart had never left the foggy banks of the Thames.

Years passed, and Judy published paper after paper upon the habits of giant river kraken, forcing the town of London to stand up and take notice. Under her direction, the crisis was brought under control.

Impossible to completely eliminate the tenacious creatures.

"No." She pulled away and took a deep breath. "Not one bit. My aunt's only hope of survival lives beneath the building next door."

"The one about to crumble into the canal?" he asked, his voice incredulous. "The one beneath which a giant lagoon kraken is rumored to have made its home?"

"It's no rumor."

He let out a long exhale. Of course. How could it not involve a kraken?

They'd met at Oxford — as assigned laboratory partners — to dissect various specimens of the unusual cephalopod species that had emerged from the depths of the ocean in past decades. A curious cross between squid and octopus, their origins were a mystery that cryptozoologists still struggled to comprehend. Hypotheses were many, conclusive evidence lacking.

Judy had wished to understand everything about kraken, including their place in the ecosystem. His aspirations involved the engineering of military submersibles capable of withstanding the increasing number of kraken attacks in the Adriatic Sea. Such differing perspectives had led to a number of academic arguments. Arturo's lips twitched at the memory. Passionate arguments conducted upon the narrow bed of a residence hall while wearing few, if any, clothes.

Years ago, they'd let their careers separate them. He set his jaw. He'd not let it happen again.

She took a deep breath, yanking his thoughts back to the present. "You worked for the Navy for a number of years, and you've experience with both diving and kraken."

With effort, he lightened his voice, attempting a teasing tone. The thought of climbing into that canal made him feel as if he'd swallowed a handful of screws. "You're telling me I've volunteered to battle a sea kraken? Underwater?"

A flash of relief and gratitude washed across her face. "With proper preparation, there should be no reason for it to turn into a battle."

Her eyes held so much hope, he wished he could tell her he slew the beasts regularly in their underwater grottos. Alas. "Yes to the diving, but I've no practice at hand-to-tentacle combat."

"Nor have I." The faintest of smiles tugged at her lips.

"We'll do our best not to begin today. Come. There's much I've not been permitted to tell you." Judy caught his hand, threading her fingers through his, and warmth rushed through him. He loved that sense of connectedness whenever they were... intertwined. "We don't want to *kill* the giant kraken, just stun her. Her presence in the Cannaregio district is the reason indigo kraken are so plentiful here. Lord Garrick bought that building when he realized she'd burrowed beneath it, then hired me."

His lips twisted. "It can't be allowed to happen to another building, Judy. If the pilings are damaged..."

"It will eventually collapse," she finished. "I know. Which is why we need to figure out how to keep these kraken alive in an aquarium. Once that is accomplished," she waved her free hand in the air, "then your bladed gates are Venice's best hope to reach some sort of equilibrium wherein small kraken can coexist with water traffic."

She led him down a staircase to the *fondaco*, the ground floor, where a long hall paved with red Verona marble served as her laboratory. Workbenches lined the hall's length, supporting — every few feet — a glass aquarium that could hold fifty-five gallons of seawater. Only three were filled.

At the far end was the *porta d'acqua*, the water entrance, a point of access rarely opened in Venice anymore.

There, her laboratory assistant Vittoria was busy assembling equipment Judy would need to dive in the canal — a suit, a helmet, air hose, an air compressor and weapons. Thank aether she included weapons.

"We'll need an extra suit, Vittoria," Judy called. "We've added a canal expert to our team."

He pulled his shoulders back at the hint of pride in her voice. Not since university had she welcomed him inside her academic sphere.

"Excellent," Vittoria called back. A grin split her face for she'd been championing his suit ever since he presented Judy with an autographed copy of *Into the Aphotic Depths: The Biology of the Vampyromorphidia*. "A moment, if you will, for me to tug it from storage." She disappeared through a doorway into a smaller storage room. Sounds of rummaging emerged.

"Kraken spawn in the spring months," he stated, turning back to the aquariums and lifting an eyebrow. "It's May. I would think the tanks would be full."

"That's the problem," Judy admitted. "Despite our best efforts, hatchling survival rate is extremely low. There's some critical element they require in their environment that we haven't been able to mimic."

He squinted at the murky water in the tank with a frown. An eye stared back at him, then a long, sinuous tentacle — tipped with a razor-sharp hook — threaded through the narrow-gauge wire mesh capping the tank, reaching... hunting.

He suppressed a shudder.

In captivity, kraken had to be securely caged as they had shown a disturbing tendency to wander. A Venetian nobleman had met a particularly gruesome fate the night his servants neglected to secure the *porta d'acqua* one night.

Tales of a mucilaginous trail through the palazzo — leading to, or perhaps from, his bed — had gripped the imagination of the locals as family members launched a futile search for their missing relative.

"How many kraken?"

"Ten," Judy said. "But two have grown ill. The pH of their tank is rising daily despite extreme buffering."

"An ink shortage," he concluded. "You're hunting a giant kraken to relieve her of her ink."

"Exactly. Both quality and quantity count. I have neither."

Though her words were strong, she fidgeted with the lace on her sleeve. Did she still wonder if he would abandon her? A sane man would, but he was a man in love and that made him a fool. Not that he'd change a thing. Into the canal he would go. "I gather the processed product is reduced several times over in volume?"

With a relieved exhale, she led him across the hall. "We refine it using this device, the Giordano Restorative Apparatus."

Crouched against the wall, a hammered-brass alembic pot sprouted coils of brass tubing. There were numerous vents, knobs and dials. At the far end of the appliance a spigot was positioned above a small spout ready to pour its magical elixir into the nearby collection vials that waited patiently, neatly queued in a wire rack.

She closed her eyes, and spoke with simmering resentment. "Much as I hate it, Lord Garrick has refused to fund in vitro experiments and has instead leapt directly to human trials."

"The ink has been... injected directly into humans?" Arturo frowned.

Her nod was stiff. "That's why I travel to Rome so frequently. Lord Garrick's personal physician chooses from among his patients."

"And those wealthy enough to afford such experimental care refuse to travel." He shook his head slowly with disappointment.

"I know," she said, reading the disappointment in his eyes. "I've every intention to make this treatment available to those without deep pockets; we *must* be able to maintain indigo kraken in captivity. Meanwhile, my work has slipped into an ethically gray area. I had to go behind his back to collaborate with Dr. Fracastoro. If Lord Garrick finds out... Well. Now we know what he's capable of."

"Dr. Fracastoro?"

"A chemist in Rome. It's the addition of his adjuvant — a chemical agent — to the ink, that halted the growth and spread of three very different cancers."

"Impressive." His jaw fell open. "But you said halt, not cure."

"I know, I know. But you can see how I must try." Judy took a deep breath. "If I don't try, then the cancerous tendrils wrapped about my aunt's spine *will* kill her. My aunt is out of time."

Arturo cupped her face and pressed a kiss to her forehead. "We'll do everything we can."

Vittoria re-emerged from the storage closet, adding a second dive suit and all its accoutrements to the pile. Reluctantly, he let Judy go.

"Hunting indigo kraken from the canals is not a possibility?" he asked. Diving in the canals was insanity, diving beneath a collapsing building... He suppressed a shudder.

"No." Judy unclasped the necklace that hung about her throat. "Once the ink is removed from its sac, or the animal dies, the quality of the ink begins to degrade." Her earrings landed on the workbench beside the necklace.

He had to tear his gaze away from the delicate skin of her throat. "And the giant kraken you intend to stalk has the largest, best quality of ink."

"Exactly."

Lagoon kraken reached sexual maturity when they measured seven feet, beak to fin. "Dare I ask the size of this beast?"

"I estimate she should be between twelve and fifteen feet in length, excluding tentacles."

Aether. Only through a thick pane of glass had he glimpsed a creature of such a large size. The screws in his stomach began to turn. He scraped his fingers through his still-damp hair. "Please tell me you have a way to subdue this kraken."

She started. "Of course." Placing a hand on his arm, she added, "I wouldn't allow you to follow me to certain death."

A small comfort.

"The equipment is ready, Professor Ravensburg," Vittoria called from the far end of the hall. But she didn't join them, for she was already reaching to unbolt the lock that barred the *porta d'acqua* against the kraken.

Time to go.

"If you wouldn't mind," she said, presenting the back of her corset, laughing when her backward glance caught a glimpse of his reddening face.

"I mind only the circumstances that force you to disrobe." His fingers paused as he glanced at Vittoria. "And the lack of privacy." He cleared his throat and focused on loosening her laces.

"There's no time to lose. If — when — Lord Garrick discovers the presence of both you and my aunt, my plan will no longer be an option." She tossed her corset aside and began to unlace her bodice. His eyebrows nearly touched his hairline when — with a quick tug — the heavy, dark material of her gown slid to the floor in a heap. She turned to face him wearing nothing but filmy undergarments and ankle boots. His gaze fell from her face, recalling how she used to like it when he — No. Not the time for such thoughts. Her voice shook for the briefest moment, but then was once again all business. "Indigo kraken are nocturnal and because we'll be swimming through a narrow opening into an unknown space beneath an unstable structure —"

"And we have two hours left of slack water," Arturo finished. His own calculations this morning had revolved around the shifting of the lagoon tides.

"Let's suit up, then I'll show you how to operate our Frommholtz spray gun. I've loaded it with an — as of today — no-longer-proprietary squid tranquilizer."

He brightened. "Water soluble?" The oil-based chemical they used at work sites only discouraged the beasts from surfacing. Imagine the progress they could make if they could completely immobilize the kraken. And that bastard Lord Garrick had been keeping it all to himself, probably looking to sell it to the highest bidder.

"Of course. You keep the creatures quiet, and I'll collect the ink. We'll be in and out in thirty minutes." Turning on a heel, she lifted an enormous syringe from a workbench and strode toward the *porta d'acqua* where her assistant waited, dive suit in hand.

CHAPTER FOUR

Judy's fingers fumbled with the clasp as she buckled the dive belt about her waist. A proper woman would avert her eyes from the tantalizing view before her, but she was anything but proper. Besides, they'd once shared a bed.

Time had wrought splendid changes, highlighted by the damp clothing that clung to his powerful form as he climbed into the dive suit. Always strong, his muscles were now forged bands of iron. The planes of his face, dark and weathered from hours upon the lagoon beneath the Italian sun, seemed sharper. At Oxford, he'd shaved, but she rather preferred him with a close-cropped beard, a rough brush against her skin that set her body ablaze with every kiss.

His eyes were the same. Dark and glinting, they saw through her tough, professional exterior in a way no one else ever had. Buried deep inside her heart, there was never any chance another man could take his place. Many had tried and failed.

She'd accepted this research position, hoping their paths would cross again, and from the moment her gaze fell upon the man he'd become, her heart rate had spiked. Her entire body ached for his touch. Even now. The heated stare he'd given her as she undressed... She fanned her face and struggled to recall why she'd not yet taken him to her bed. Again. The moment this was behind them, at the very first opportunity that presented itself, she promised herself she would do exactly that.

A wave of Arturo's jet-black hair fell across his forehead as he bent to grasp the dive suit — and caught her looking. He grinned. "The things I do for the woman I love."

Love. There was that word again, last whispered between them one dark and fateful night. A lump formed in her throat. Was it possible, after all these years?

"Vittoria," he said when she failed to reply. "If you'll give us a moment?"

Cheeks pink, Vittoria cleared her throat. "Of course. There's an air filter I should fetch from the storage room." She hurried away.

"Come." Arturo beckoned, his gaze growing serious.

Judy hesitated. Her heart pounded. "This isn't the best time —"

"Always running, Judith." He stepped closer to her. "Grant me five minutes, then we will accomplish the not-quite impossible task of stalking a giant kraken in its underwater lair." He caught her chin between his thumb and forefinger. "It's time to settle things between us. It's true. I wanted you to be the mother of my children. But more than that, I wanted you by my side." The pad of his thumb stroked across her lips. Tears of happiness gathered in her eyes. "I'm sorry for leaving you as I did. Perhaps things could have been different. I've never stopped loving you. When I think of a woman at my side, I can only envision you."

What little oxygen remained in her lungs fled. She placed her hand against the side of his cheek, brushing her palm over its rough surface and blinked back tears. "And I you."

He fell to one knee.

Now? Here? What a sight they must be, dressed in their dive suits, standing beside a pile of hoses and a hand-crank air compressor. Her knees grew weak.

"Will you — the moment this crisis is behind us — will you marry me?" he began. "My house is nowhere this grand, but it does lie upon a canal. Indigo kraken *have* been pulled from its waters. My *fondaco* is yours to fill with as many kraken as can be managed, and the hospital is only a few doors away. I'm certain they won't object to the saving of lives."

His eyes pleaded with her. It was impossible to deny him, to deny herself a second time. Bending over, she caught his lips with her own, pouring her love into their kiss. For the first time in years, her heart sang with the promise of the future.

"Yes," she said a long moment later, smiling down at him

as unshed tears of happiness gathered in her eyes. "I'll marry you. Without delay."

"Signor! Signorina!" Vittoria called, smiling as she pressed a hand to her heart. A romantic, she'd championed Arturo's return to Judy's life from the moment he'd appeared at her dock-side lecture. "If you're to dive today..."

Arturo stood, smoothing Judy's tousled hair back behind her ears, his smile broadening as he handed her a dive helmet. "I am the happiest of men." He waved a hand at the *porta d'acqua*. "I am familiar with the equipment, but you are the cryptobiologist, the expert on indigo kraken behavior. What is the best approach?"

She —*they* — were really going to do this. Dive. Marry. Her heart — already racing — began to pound harder. "Only once before have I entered a kraken grotto," she began. "It's... unpleasant." To enter one fashioned by a beast beneath a building that might — at any moment — crumble into the canal? Her stomach ached, but it needed to be done. She would save her aunt... then worry about extricating herself from Lord Garrick's clutches and marrying her lifelong love. "They use their hooks to scrape and claw at mud, wood and even stone, until they create a large enough space to hang their eggs."

"Hang?" A bit of the color left Arturo's face.

She nodded, a corner of her mouth twitching at his squeamishness. "We swim at the water's surface until we reach the damaged house. Vittoria will cover us until that point. Then we submerge. From what we can tell, the kraken has tunneled through the canal mud to reach the building's foundations. I expect to find an opening gouged through and between the pilings edging the canal."

He whistled. "That would explain the crack across the building's *façade*."

"I estimate the tunnel will be approximately five feet wide, given the warping of the building's floor. It likely continues some four feet into the foundations, before widening."

"You'll enter first, Mr. Piatti, to neutralize the kraken." Vittoria handed Arturo a modified Frommholtz spray gun. "Pull this lever and it will shoot some fifty pellets a distance of eight to ten feet. The water will activate the squid tranquilizer in approximately ten seconds."

He frowned. "Not instantaneously?"

"Not even the richest Brit in Venice has been able to improve upon this design." Vittoria twisted her lips. "Plan accordingly."

"These are the only extra cartridges we have," Judy added, clipping two more to the D-rings of his dive belt. "Tempting as it is to fire upon the kraken in the canal to clear our path, we need to save the cartridges for the grotto, where the hydrophobic cephalopod-stunning oil will have no effect."

"Noted," Arturo said. "I've no interest in tangling with the tentacles of a fifteen-foot indigo lagoon kraken."

"Ready?" Vittoria asked.

"Almost," Judy answered. She examined her over-large syringe one last time, then stowed it in its protective leather case and clipped it onto her own dive belt. They had one chance at this. If the glass casing broke or the needle snapped, her aunt's life was forfeit. She set her jaw. Aunt Agatha *needed* to be at her wedding. Shoving doubts and concerns aside, she hoisted a perforated canister from the defensive supplies stockpiled beside the *porta d'acqua* and gave a sharp nod. "All set."

Vittoria hoisted a rifle to her shoulder and threw open the water gates. Sunlight streamed inward and a breeze carrying a hint of salt blew through the room. Outside, the water of the canal roiled and bubbled as a kraken surfaced, reaching with a glistening tentacle to snatch a gull from the sky.

Crack!

A squawk. A splash. A widening ripple of waves. The gull struggled to the surface, once again taking to the air.

Arturo's jaw dropped as he stared at Vittoria. The usual reaction when men discovered her petite assistant had such deadly aim. "Luigi would love to add you to his team," he said. "Should you want to change the trajectory of your career —"

"Don't even think about trying to steal her away," Judy interrupted with a faint smile. She stepped forward and tossed a perforated canister onto the water, waiting as the oily cephalopod-stunning substance oozed from its many holes. A nerve irritant, it sent all but the most determined kraken back into the mud.

"Keep your heads above water until you reach the drop point while I watch for any large kraken moving in your direction." With the toss of a match, Vittoria ignited the burner of the air pump. A mechanical roar filled the room.

"I'll lead us to the opening, but you'll enter first to tranquilize the giant kraken," Judy yelled to Arturo over the noise. "Once activated, the tranquilizer will work for ten minutes. That ought to be enough time."

"If it's not?" Arturo bellowed back.

"Fire again!" Judy yelled. "You have three rounds!" She dropped the dive helmet over her head, clipped it in place, then slid slowly and carefully into the canal trusting him to follow.

CHAPTER FIVE

THIS WAS INSANE. *He* was insane. His fiancée was insane.

Fiancée. He smiled inside his dive helmet as he half-floated, half-climbed along the side of a building edging the canal. Perhaps insanity wasn't such a bad thing.

Impossible not to think about the integrity of Venice's foundations. The entire city rested upon some ten million ancient tree trunks that had been pounded into mud and clay. In such oxygen-poor conditions, they'd been safe for hundreds of years. Until this particular indigo kraken dug through the canal sediment, damaging the pilings. If other indigo kraken reached full maturity and adopted the behavioral pattern of building their grottos beneath buildings, Venice was doomed.

That thought wiped the smile from his face.

A quick, tentative tapping upon his thigh, and then a

sinuous tentacle snaked about his ankle. Even as his hand fell upon his dive knife, the creature yanked, dipping his shoulders into the water. Heart racing as a second tug pulled him underwater, he sliced through the tentacle. An eddy of water swirled about him as he kicked back to the surface.

Crack!

He glanced back at Vittoria who lowered her rifle and gave him a thumbs up. Taking a deep breath, he confirmed that his airline was undamaged. So far, he'd escaped the razor-sharp claws. He prayed they'd not encounter them today. Judy had paused, but he waved her forward. Only five feet more to go. Turning back was not an option.

If not for Lord Garrick's actions and not-so-veiled threats, this mission could have been better organized, staffed and executed. Despite Vittoria's marksmanship and the oily cephalopod-stunning substance coating the water's surface, a drag net and his own sharpshooters would have been welcome additions.

But it was time to set such musings aside and focus on the task at hand. They'd reached the front of the crumbling building.

"Ready?" He read Judy's lips through the circular glass window.

He gave her a nod. Flipping on the bioluminescent head-lamp built into the dive helmet — another costly feature funded by ill-gotten gains — he readied the modified Frommholtz spray gun and submerged.

Judy's light lowered into position beside him. For a long minute they hung, suspended in the water, united by their apprehension as they waited for their eyes to adjust to the murky gloom.

The light from his headlamp cast a blue-white glow that penetrated into the muddy tunnel a mere three feet in front of them. Pushing his booted feet gently against the canal floor, he drifted into the passage, weapon at the ready.

A moment later, pilings began to appear beside him. He paused, taking in his surroundings.

Uncanny to rest his eyes on the trunks that supported his city. Those at the edge of the opening — though still largely intact — bore the scars of the hooks that must tear at them every time the creatures entered or exited. Inside, drifting in the calm water, he could just make out the tips of faint, pinkish-white tentacles capped with deadly hooks.

Every muscle tensed in readiness. But they were here to preserve life today, not end it. Still, he promised himself that not another building's foundations would house a giant kraken. Somehow, the indigo kraken would breed in captivity if he had to spend all of his time figuring out what exactly the tanks lacked.

At the edge of his vision, something caught his attention. He turned, redirecting his light. A man-made device — with a dial set into its metal housing — was fixed to one of the wooden pilings just inside the opening. Wires ran outward, twisting and twining as they disappeared into the black depths of the grotto. A monitoring device.

Lord Garrick had deliberately kept her in the dark. A ripple of uneasiness ran down his spine.

With a wave of his hand, Arturo directed Judy's attention to the instrument. Together, they swam closer. He squinted, trying to determine what exactly the needle — currently pointing to zero — indicated. Impossible to know.

He faced Judy again, lifting his eyebrows, silently asking her opinion. She replied with a shake of her head and an upturned hand. Hard to read her expression in the dim light, but he thought her lips pressed together into an irritated line, but it wasn't enough to make her turn back. No doubt he would hear about it in great detail once they surfaced.

She pointed a finger at his weapon, then into the depths of the cavern, indicating she wished to proceed as planned. He drifted forward. Lifting the Frommholtz, he aimed at the center of the grotto and fired.

With a *whomp*, felt more than heard, the cartridge disappeared into the blackness. Tentacles twitched, then fell still, drifting with the slow motion of the water currents once again. He counted as the seconds passed, but the tentacles didn't move again.

Water shifted and swirled as Judy unhooked her giant syringe and uncapped a needle the length of his forearm. He replaced the cartridge of the Frommholtz. With his thumbs up, she moved deeper into the cave. He followed.

Caged on every side by disintegrating pilings and lit with the blue-white light of their headlamps, the cavernous space was eerie. Tentacles drifted, ending in sharp hooks, and he and Judy followed their lengths, a terrifying path toward the beast. Kraken claws wrought havoc upon all they touched, but the sharp beak at its mouth was deadly. Moving deeper, her offspring became visible.

At the edges of the den, white globules dangled upon strings, clustering one beside the other to form a kind of disturbing curtain that drifted back and forth in the gentle water currents. Inside the many protuberances — the thousands of egg cases — baby kraken stirred. His skin crawled.

Careful not to disturb any egg cases, they moved forward until they came upon the mother kraken. A giant eye stared at them, unseeing, while water jetted slowly forth from a siphon at the edge of her mantle. Arturo took a deep breath, steadying his nerves, and raised the Frommholtz. With only two rounds left, he didn't want to fire unless it was absolutely necessary.

Judy approached carefully, tapping the kraken's pinkish-white mantle with her gloved fingertip. No response, not even the slightest twitch of movement. Excellent. She directed the sharp tip of her needle to a location just behind the siphon, aiming for the creature's internal ink sac.

As the steel pierced the kraken's mantle, he struggled to keep his breathing steady. His fiancée was a dauntless woman.

Judy hesitated, readjusted her angle, and finally pulled back on the plunger. A thick, dark liquid swirled into the glass barrel. With some two-hundred cubic centiliters of ink collected, she re-capped the syringe. Once it had been returned to the protective case and clipped to her dive belt, she gestured that it was time to go. *Thank the aether.*

Ever so gradually they backed away.

A dull *thud* reverberated through the water. He jerked

around, his gaze landing upon the device strapped to the entry. The needle quivered, pointing to the number seven.

The giant kraken began to stir. Grabbing Judy's arm, he pushed her into the mud tunnel and turned to follow.

A tentacle lashed out, catching him about the ankle, yanking him backward into the kraken's lair. Another hooked tentacle caught at Judy's dive suit. Adrenaline flooded his bloodstream as he twisted, pointing, shooting another cartridge at the mother kraken. But not before its hook sliced through Judy's dive suit and into her skin, releasing a small trickle of blood. His pulse raced. She jerked, but he couldn't see her face through the murky water.

Even the smallest of the kraken would stir to the smell and the taste of human blood in the water, daylight be damned, leaving the mud in hopes of an easy meal. No choice but to rush back to the palazzo's *porta d'acqua* and escape the canal.

Not that they would make it if the creature followed. The tentacle about his leg loosened, but didn't release. He loaded the last cartridge and fired. Throwing the Frommholtz aside, he untangled the now-limp tentacle from his calf, then turned to follow Judy into the mud-encased tunnel, relieved to notice the injury hadn't yet slowed her movements.

A slow, disturbing creak sounded through the chamber — the wooden planks resting overhead upon the pilings ruptured, their splintered ends caving into the chamber. A stone fell with a *thunk* into the mud. Panic clawed at his throat as he swam for the exit.

A wave of water gushed past and the ominous groan of over-stressed wood echoed through the space. He kicked hard, pulling himself through the water. Ahead, Judy disappeared from view. He was almost there...

CHAPTER SIX

HEART POUNDING, Judy slid free from the mud tunnel into the canal and surfaced. Pain from the kraken's claws blossomed across her leg, but it was a minor cut. The greater risk came from the slow, but steady, influx of canal water trickling into her suit. She patted the syringe — still fastened to her belt — then reached for the brick wall of the building, pulling herself hand over hand as fast as possible back toward the palazzo. Already the canal water roiled with kraken — flailing tentacles bumped against her hips and legs. Though confused by the overhead sun filtering into their sensitive eyes and deterred by the slick of squid tranquilizer floating upon the water, they scented blood. A call they could not ignore.

She glanced behind her and hesitated. Where was Arturo? He'd been right behind her when that horrible creak of stressed wood had reverberated through the cavernous space making every single hair on the back of her neck quiver.

Unease gripped her stomach. Was it worse than she thought? Had a beam fallen free, trapping him underneath the building?

Reversing course, she headed back, ignoring the risk that any blood oozing from her thigh might attract more kraken.

That device. Someone had been beneath the house at Lord Garrick's behest, for he'd certainly not gone himself. At first she'd thought he'd placed it merely to monitor the severity of the building's instability, but what if it had been wired to cause a cave-in? But how? Why?

She had nearly returned to the mud tunnel when a tremor ran through her.

No.

Beneath her hands.

Plop. A brick splashed into the water beside her. Another. Beneath her fingers, the building she gripped shuddered, and a shower of bricks rained down.

The building was collapsing.

She screamed. *Arturo!*

Splashing water obscured her view as brick after brick fell from the crumbling building. Tiles slid from the roof. Glass shattered. A balcony began to give way. She kicked, dodging the falling debris.

Submerging, praying nothing would strike her directly, she frantically searched... but nowhere in the disaster could she find Arturo, and the water was growing murkier by the second as bricks fell and splashed. Panic overwhelmed her and a desperate need for oxygen clawed at her chest. She tried to drag in a deep breath — but there was no air!

Had the falling building severed her air hose?

Clutching the clasps that held her helmet to her suit, she kicked for the surface, but a tug yanked her head sideways. Another jerk set her in motion, pulling her both upward and back toward the palazzo. Not severed then. The pump must have failed, and Vittoria was dragging her to safety.

Her lungs screamed, and spots danced before her eyes. *Arturo!* Too many years they'd spent apart, lived entire lives without each other. She wanted to marry him, to know that he was at last hers. He had to be alive. Her fingers fumbled on the latches. Removing her helmet would mean she couldn't re-enter the tunnel, but she couldn't leave him...

Vaguely, Judy was aware she'd broke the surface. Strong hands gripped her shoulders, hauling her over algae-covered steps and through the *porta d'acqua* onto the floor. Someone wrenched her dive helmet free.

Gasping, she gulped air. Lord Garrick's visage swam into view overhead. There was a tug at her waist, and he straightened, her overlarge syringe in hand. She prayed the glass barrel wouldn't shatter; it was her aunt's only hope. But there was a more pressing problem.

"There's a man. Under the collapsing building. We have to help him!" She tried to stand. But the grasp on her shoulders wouldn't allow it. The steam butler held her tightly in his jointed grip. "Battista, release me! We need to turn the air pump back on!"

"I'm afraid Battista will no longer be responding to your

commands." Lord Garrick carefully placed the syringe upon a workbench, then tugged a handkerchief from his pocket and began to meticulously dry his hands.

"What!" She shoved a wet lock of hair from her face. "My fiancé —"

"Mr. Piatti is *not* on the list of authorized individuals, affianced or not. Whatever made you think you could share proprietary information with him without consequence?" He tossed the linen square aside, while turning the full bite of his angry gaze upon her. "It matters not if he survives the building's collapse — more convenient if he dies. I can't have him shutting down this operation prematurely."

Her heartbeat thrashed loudly in her ears. This could not be happening. She pried at Battista's unyielding fingers.

"A more pertinent question becomes: where do your loyalties lie, Lady Judith?" He shook his head and tsked. "You are in violation of the terms of our contract." On the workbench beside her syringe sat her precious tea canister. "Did you think I wouldn't find out about your collaboration with Dr. Fracastoro? About this adjuvant you've transported here in an unusually large quantity?"

Judy gulped.

"We agreed the giant kraken would remain undisturbed so as to provide new generations of indigo hatchlings. Moreover, you brought an unsanctioned guest into *my* house. Did you seek permission to treat your aunt? No. And then I learn that you have taken it upon yourself to visit the kraken's lair so that you might personally benefit, sparing no thought for others, including Vittoria."

His hand waved. Her eyes followed its sweep. Ten feet away, Vittoria was propped against the wall, bound and gagged, her eyes wide. True to form, she struggled against the ropes that held her.

Speech failed her. Tears streamed down her face. How did one reason with a man willing to kill so casually? She had drastically underestimated his mercenary inclinations.

"Good. At last you begin to grasp the situation." Lord Garrick leaned backward against a wall, crossing his arms while Arturo drowned.

Judy strove for control. Weeping would solve nothing. She fought the steambot's grip, but to no avail. She cast about for a makeshift weapon. There, Vittoria's harpoon gun. It lay a few inches past her booted foot. She shifted. Maybe if she could hook it with her heel. If Lord Garrick looked away...

"Foreseeing your altruistic tendencies, I had the building rigged," he stated. The calm amusement in his voice made her want to scream. "Any attempt to enter using the Frommholtz cartridges would trigger a chemical sensor and, consequently, a number of explosives."

"You blew up the building?" She gulped. "On purpose? But that's where the mother kraken lives!"

"Come now, you're smarter than that." Lord Garrick cocked his head. "Did you think that creature was the only sexually mature indigo kraken in Venice? My men have located two more kraken actively digging grottos." He shrugged. "Besides, it won't do to saturate the market with indigo ink. Greater profit lies in developing a treatment for tumors, not in providing a cure."

Profits.

Trickle out the treatment. Keep sick individuals paying, scrounging for money, perhaps squandering their life savings or turning to lives of crime while other needs went unmet. All so that an already rich man could enlarge his coffers. "That's horrible! You're already as rich as Croesus!"

Lord Garrick smiled, unmoved, as he paced across the room to the Giordano Restorative Apparatus. "It's the nature of the business. I don't suppose you'll agree to cooperate?"

Out of the corner of her eye, she saw a small movement. There, to the side of the *porta d'acqua,* just beyond Lord Garrick's line of sight, a diving helmet. *Arturo!*

She inhaled sharply, then froze. Drawing attention to him almost guaranteed his death. Instead, she lifted her chin. "Why should I?"

Arturo pulled the helmet from his head. The portal glass was cracked and his face was grim, but he was alive. Relief washed over her. She would see he stayed that way.

"Because you're either with me or you're against me. If you agree to let your aunt meet a natural death," Lord Garrick said, absently polishing the already gleaming copper pot, "I will agree not to toss you back into the canal to share the same watery, tentacle-laden grave as your fiancé."

Holding her breath, Judy waited for the moment his eyes were averted and kicked out, sending Vittoria's harpoon gun hurling over the edge of the *porta d'acqua.* Arturo's arm thrust out, catching it. At the same time, she lashed out against Battista, struggling in his iron grip, kicking and thrashing, making as much noise as she could.

Alerted by the commotion, Lord Garrick turned back to her. And went rigid. "Well, well, well. A complication." His posture relaxed once more as — like a fool — he walked *toward* Arturo, rather than away, to stand at the threshold and stare down at him. "Mr. Piatti won't shoot."

"Don't be so sure about that," Arturo growled.

"Should I die," Lord Garrick drawled. "Battista will enact protocol 523." The steam butler's cold fingers encircled her throat. "Your fiancée will end up in the canal with you. In pieces. Where the kraken will conveniently dispose of all evidence." The corners of his lips curled up.

"Bastard," she hissed.

Bang!

With a whoosh of air, a harpoon pierced Lord Garrick's arm and drove into the chest of the steam butler. Battista's fingers released as he clattered to the floor, his master pinned to him like an insect on display, screaming in pain. Both fitting and gratifying.

She threw herself across the floor, helping Arturo, bloody, beaten and muddy, as he began to climb from the canal. Alive. He was alive.

Inches from safety, the giant kraken surfaced behind him, her eyes wild and tentacles lashing. Their sharp hooks and suckers flailed about, catching at weapons, equipment. In the blink of an eye, they found soft, warm human flesh. Flexing and coiling, they dragged Arturo and Lord Garrick into the canal.

Judy screamed, her arms still outstretched.

Arturo surfaced, spitting muddy water and gasping for air before the kraken dragged him under again.

Damned if this was how it was going to end. He'd not fought his way back through a tunnel of mud, survived a hailstorm of brick and stone, to die at the tentacles of a bloody kraken.

Hand to hip, he freed his dive knife, hacking blindly around him as the water swirled and churned. One tentacle's grip loosened and fell away only to be replaced by the sharp hook of another. On and on he fought, gulping air every time he surfaced.

Bang!

The tentacles gripping him fell away.

Bang!

He broke the water's surface. He blinked and swam for the palazzo, toward Judy who extended a long pole while Vittoria stood to her side, aiming her rifle at the many kraken swarming the canal behind him.

He lunged up the steps and fell across the threshold of the *porta d'acqua* onto the solid marble of the floor tiles. Judy dragged him forward, far away from the reach of any tentacles and wrapped her arms around him. Behind them, Vittoria spat curses in Italian as she fired upon the kraken. Or perhaps upon Lord Garrick. He lacked the will to care which.

"Aether," Judy cried, falling on her knees and dropping kisses onto his dripping hair. "Twice I thought I'd lost you."

Her hands roamed over his body, searching for any hint of damage.

"I'm fine," he said, pulling her face toward his for a long and satisfying kiss. "Mostly," he murmured into her neck. "Nothing that a few days in bed with my fiancée can't fix."

Tears streamed down her face as she laughed. "Soon. Very, very soon."

Bang!

Vittoria slammed the water access doors, barring them. "Gone," she said. A satisfied and slightly evil smile spread across her face. "He's nothing but kraken bait now."

He lay back upon the floor with a grin. "Process the ink quickly, my love. We've a life to save and a wedding to plan."

EPILOGUE

Dear Aunt Judy,

Warmest congratulations! I hear you are to be married. Uncle Arturo positively trips off the tongue. Please accept my apologies as well. It seems a number of airship passengers took my comment about Venice crumbling into the sea to heart. Those in my profession are frequently given over to extreme exaggeration, and I fear some may have become rather concerned for the welfare of a well-loved playground.

Your favorite niece,
Olivia

Her brother's children were quite the handful.

With a smile, Judy set the note aside and crossed the room to join her aunt upon the balcony of the *piano nobile*, the first floor, overlooking the canal that ran before Arturo's home. *Their* home.

"A beautiful sight, is it not?" Aunt Agatha said. Contentment radiated from her face.

"It is." For the first time in decades, gondoliers in striped shirts traveled upon its waters beneath a full moon. One gondolier caught sight of them above, waved, and broke into song. Thanks to Arturo's *I Cancelli di Recupero del Canale*, three canals were now safe. More would follow.

Every day this district of Venice showed new signs of life. Flowers appeared in window boxes. Laundry hung from clotheslines. A vegetable cart arrived in the *campo* — square — beside the church where she and Arturo had spoken their vows earlier today.

Below, in her new laboratory, a small indigo lagoon kraken resided in a ten-gallon tank. Promising, even if its constant testing of the locked lid with its hooks was somewhat worrisome.

"No pain, numbness?" Judy asked, hardly able to believe her mad scheme had worked.

Aunt Agatha reached out and squeezed her hand. "Nothing. Even my ancient joints feel ten years younger."

While the population of Venice gawked at the collapse of one of their ancient buildings, wringing its collective hands, Judy and Vittoria — urged onward by Arturo — had set the Giordano Restorative Apparatus into motion, frantically processing the indigo ink with Dr. Fracastoro's adjuvant. Mere hours after their perilous diving expedition, Judy had stood beside her aunt's bed to administer the first injection.

As the days passed, Arturo fended off city officials and men seeking the unaccountably missing Lord Garrick. He directed his project from her palazzo, venturing out only to visit Gino in the hospital where — mercifully — his hand had been saved. Slowly but steadily, Aunt Agatha also recovered. Though it was impossible to be certain the tumor was in complete remission, there was no evidence to the contrary.

At the soft sound of footfalls on the floor behind her, Judy smiled. Moments later Arturo's strong arms wrapped around her waist, pulling her tight against his hard form.

"Enjoying the view from *our* home, Signoria Piatti?" he murmured into her neck before nipping it playfully.

Heat rushed through her veins. "I am, husband." Arturo claimed fate had brought them back together, but knowing he was in Venice had certainly swayed her decision to study its lagoon kraken. Some small part of her had hoped a spark might once again flare between them.

And it most definitely had.

"I do believe I'll retire for the night," her aunt announced. "It's been a trial, bringing you two together once more, but at least my illness served some purpose."

"Rather dramatic," Arturo agreed, releasing Judy long enough to kiss Aunt Agatha upon each cheek. "But Judy has been telling stories about her nieces, and peril before matrimony seems to be a family trait."

"That it does." With a low laugh, Aunt Agatha departed, leaving them alone upon the balcony.

"Where were we?" Arturo nuzzled her neck as his hands loosened the laces of her bodice. "Beautiful as your wedding gown is, I can't wait any longer to reach the woman beneath."

His hands began to wander, and her hands caught at the stone balcony as her knees threatened to give out. She uttered a half-hearted protest. "We should retire to our room."

But her husband was committed to his undertaking. "In a minute..."

ABOUT THE AUTHOR

Though ANNE RENWICK holds a Ph.D. in biology and greatly enjoyed tormenting the overburdened undergraduates who were her students, fiction has always been her first love. Today, she writes steampunk romance, placing a new kind of biotech in the hands of mad scientists, proper young ladies and determined villains.

Anne brings an unusual perspective to steampunk. A number of years spent locked inside the bowels of a biological research facility left her permanently altered. In her steampunk world, the Victorian fascination with all things anatomical led to a number of alarming biotechnological advances. Ones that the enemies of Britain would dearly love to possess.

www.AnneRenwick.com

instagram.com/anne_renwick
facebook.com/AnneRenwickAuthor
pinterest.com/AuthorAnneRenwick

www.ingramcontent.com/pod-product-compliance
Lightning Source LLC
Chambersburg PA
CBHW032043180726
48284CB00008B/2728